Clarty Jim McCloud

Story and illustrations
by Tim Archbold

BC

This is a tough and true story,
so you might want to sit down.

Along a rusty river,
across a coal-black bridge . . .

. . . under a stinky smog,
over a sloppy sludge . . .

. . . through a twisty tangle,
down a dirty ditch . . .

. . . past a pongy pond,
beneath a murky mist . . .

in a jumbled house of junk
lived Clarty Jim McCloud.

You would not choose to go there for a holiday.

Clarty Jim had wet feet and muddy clothes, but he was not a smelly boy. He loved puddles and ponds and streams and rivers; he loved fish and frogs and birds and beetles. Clarty Jim knew all about watery things.

He lived with his granny in the jumbled house she had built from odds and ends and bits and pieces.

Granny McCloud was a tough old lady. She did not have cats or fancy china cups, but she was kind to Clarty Jim, and he was a helpful boy.

Granny was a cook. She worked in a hot and steamy kitchen for the **SHOVE & BARGEFORTH IRONWORK COMPANY**.

Sir Humphrey Shove and Sir George Bargeforth owned the enormous
ironworks. They were very important and famous for making grand gates
and royal railings and lovely lampposts and beautiful bridges. But . . .

. . . the ironwork company also made a rusty, twisty, smoky, stinky, murky mess. Clarty Jim knew because he lived in the middle of it.

Every day before he walked to school, Granny McCloud made a big sandwich for Clarty Jim. 'Fill you up nicely,' she said.

Unfortunately, Granny made tough and terrible sandwiches for the tough and terrible men at the ironworks. They loved her cooking and the great big sandwiches they called granny-pieces.

On MONDAY she made fat skimmings and thin scrapings.

On TUESDAY she boiled up bone-jelly ends.

On WEDNESDAY she minced off-cuts.

On THURSDAY she spread blue cheese on green tomatoes.

On FRIDAY she pickled brown mashings and yellow peelings.

On SATURDAY, Clarty Jim and Granny ate thick, steamed leftovers.

On SUNDAY, just for a treat, Granny made skurdle with trotter gravy.

'A lovely piece for you, Clarty Jim,' said Granny McCloud, giving him a friendly wink.

Granny wrapped the sandwich in old newspaper and stuffed the muckle thing into his pocket.

'Thank you, Granny,' said Clarty Jim, because he was polite and did not grumble.

He walked to school along the rusty river and around the pongy pond, but he stopped on the coal-black bridge.

Clarty Jim wiped his nose on his sleeve.
He looked this way and that way and then . . .
He dropped the sandwich into the water.

PLOOP!

The sandwich sank slowly.

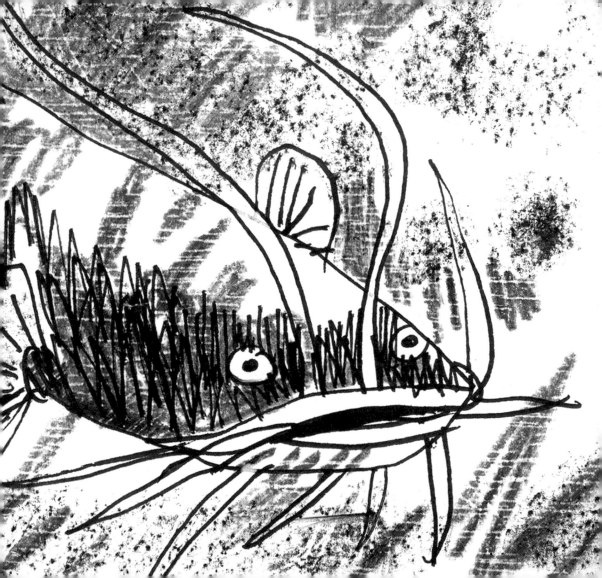

Now, you might wait for an important letter to be delivered to your house. You might watch for special friends to arrive.

Deep down in the dirty water, a great catfish watched and waited for the important and special sandwich to arrive.

('How can a sandwich be special and important?' you say. Well, this is a true story, and the fish did not receive any letters, and he had already eaten his friends, so the sandwich was important and special to him.)

The catfish had eaten all of the unfortunate fish.

He had eaten all of the fresh frogs and tasty tadpoles.

He had eaten all of the daft ducks and delicious ducklings.

So he waited every day for Clarty Jim and his sandwich.

Of course, Clarty Jim knew about the catfish. He knew what was what in the water. He had dropped his sandwich over the bridge every day for a long time.

The catfish loved the tough and terrible sandwiches.

He loved the skimmings and the scrapings and all the mashed-up, boiled-up steamed stuff crammed into Granny McCloud's pieces.

BUT this was the last day and the last sandwich.

(Listen carefully to the next bit – it's important.)

It was Clarty Jim's birthday. He was nine years old, and that meant no more school. It was time to work for the **SHOVE & BARGEFORTH IRONWORK COMPANY** because there was no one else to work for.

(Don't make that funny face. You see, long ago children had to work. Sitting on the sofa eating crisps had not been invented.)

Clarty Jim spoke softly to the catfish. 'I can't come tomorrow,' said Clarty Jim. 'But I'll save up all my granny-pieces for you. Just stay here and be good.'

He wiped his nose on his other sleeve and set off through the stink and murk.

The old catfish watched and waited, but Clarty Jim
did not come back again, and in the following days
he grew very hungry. He ate:

MUD on Monday.

TURNIP LEAVES on Tuesday.

WEEDS on Wednesday.

THREE SLUGS on Thursday.

FUZZYFLIES on Friday.

But he was still hungry. On Saturday, he set off
to find something nice and tasty.

The catfish swam up the river, away from the ironworks.
Away from the rusty, twisty, smoky, stinky, murky mess.

A farmer was filling a bucket from the river,
so the hungry catfish ate the farmer.
But UGH! He tasted dry and leathery,
so the catfish spat him out
and swam on.

A fisherman was standing in the river, so the hungry catfish ate the
fisherman. But OOOH! He tasted slippery and rubbery,
so the catfish spat him out and swam on.

A policeman was investigating a serious
report that something fishy was going on
in the river, so the catfish ate the policeman.
But OWW! He tasted sharp and pointy,
so the catfish spat him out and swam away.

Further on, where the water was clean, the catfish found
a silver stream and a perfect pond and a magnificent mansion-
house. Here there was sunshine and flowers and fresh air.

This was the home of Sir George Bargeforth. This lovely day, when the catfish arrived, was the **SHOVE & BARGEFORTH GREAT AND GRAND GARDEN PARTY**.

('Very convenient,' you say from your sofa. Well, I'm just telling you what happened. I haven't made this up. This is a true story, remember.)

This was not a garden party for the tough and terrible men at the ironworks. Sir Humphrey Shove and Sir George Bargeforth had invited only their most dainty and delicate, most impressive and important, most fabulous and famous friends.

But Clarty Jim McCloud was invited. He was the new
SHOVE & BARGEFORTH IRONWORK COMPANY
Drains (Third Class) Assistant. He was invited to clean
out the smelly drain at the back of the house.

The garden party was going wonderfully, with cream cakes and tinkly teacups and mellifluous music.

(You look it up.)

Now, Sir Humphrey's children, Miss Coco-Sugarella and her brother, Master Plum-Twistleton Shove, were in the garden, with the lovely Bargeforth baby.

They had eaten lots of cake and even more ice cream, and they began to paddle in the pond where the catfish watched and waited.

A hungry catfish cannot eat fresh air and flowers, so of course he quickly gobbled up the children and the baby.

'HELP!' cried Lady Delphinium Shove and she ran about.

'HELP!' cried Lady Margery Bargeforth and she ran about.

Sir George and Sir Humphrey ran about. 'HELP! HELP!' they wailed.

The catfish soon spat out Miss Coco-Sugarella Shove because she was too sweet.

The catfish soon spat out Master Plum-Twistleton Shove because he was too sour.

But the Bargeforth baby tasted good. Delicious as a duckling, tasty as a tadpole, fresh as a frog. Just right, thought the catfish.

Everyone ran about scattering teacups and fancy cakes.

BUT NOT Clarty Jim McCloud. He knew exactly what to do. In his bag he found five saved granny-pieces wrapped in newspaper. He quickly threw them into the water.

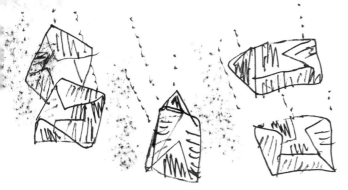

The sandwiches sank slowly.

Now, as you know, the catfish loved the skimmings and scrapings and mashings and boilings. He loved the granny-pieces more than anything, and so he decided to spit out the baby – it was beginning to have a slight nappy flavour anyway.

WEEEEEEEEEEEEEEEE!

(The baby didn't wee – that was just the sound it made as it flew through the air.)

Clarty Jim caught the baby.

HURRAH! There was a great cheer and everyone clapped and pretended they hadn't run about shouting for help.

Lady Margery hugged her happy baby and kissed Clarty Jim.

'Thank you for saving my darling baby. You will be well rewarded,' she said.

'George! Look after this fine boy, immediately!'

'Yes, dear,' bumbled Sir George.

He thanked Clarty Jim because he did love his baby.

'Now, what do you fancy?' said Sir George. 'A new hat, maybe? Some shoes, eh? How about six lampposts for your garden?'

'Or how about a bridge? We can make you a lovely bridge,' offered Sir Humphrey Shove, as he poured Clarty Jim a dainty cup of tea.

Clarty Jim did not want anything for himself. He asked only that Sir Humphrey and Sir George clean up the rusty, twisty, smoky, stinky, murky mess the **SHOVE & BARGEFORTH IRONWORK COMPANY** had made.

Lady Margery made sure this was done and she gave
Clarty Jim a medal and a new job. He was to be the
Chief River Ranger and Director of Ducks & Dragonflies,
and Foreman (First Class) for Fish & Frogs.

(I told you he knew about watery things.)

Soon, there were lots of good things in the clean water and the catfish returned to live under the bridge. He wouldn't have to eat his friends any more.

(It is never a good idea to eat your friends, no matter how good you think they might taste.)

Granny McCloud bought two cats and decided to open a small tearoom. She served dainty cakes and cream scones and also her famous tough and terrible sandwiches.

Clarty Jim planted lots of trees, and the birds came back. He grew wildflowers, and butterflies fluttered by. He cleaned out the pongy pond and made it perfect for frogs and children.

Everyone said it was a great place to go on holiday.

First published in 2016 by
BC Books, an imprint of
Birlinn Limited
West Newington House
10 Newington Road
Edinburgh
EH9 1QS

www.birlinn.co.uk

ISBN 978 1 78027 347 1

British Library Cataloguing-in-Publication Data
A catalogue record for this book is available from
the British Library

Typeset by Mark Blackadder

Printed and bound by Livonia Print, Latvia